Acknowledgements:

My constant source of inspiration, my kids: Jayvon, London and Asher-Elijah, all of whom are my favorite in their own way! Thank you for making me want to be the BEST MOST COOLEST MOM EVER and an EVEN BETTER WRITER! I love you forever & ever unconditionally!

London and Asher, sat

on the porch of their

soon to be old home

eating frozen grapes.

"Where's our new house?"

Asked Asher.

"I don't know but Momma

will figure it out!" London

said. "You know what she

always says, 'All we need

is to have faith the size

of a mustard seed.'"

"Yall ready?" Their Mother

walked out of their old

apartment carrying the last box.

"Yea, Momma let me carry that." Jayvon said, grabbing the box from his Mother.

"wait for me," Asher said, running down the porch steps. "Shotgun," London yelled to call first dibs on the front seat. "No," Momma said, "not this time. London, Jayvon's the

oldest and It's gonna be a

long ride to Syracuse.

But if Jayvon falls asleep

on me and you're still up

you get the front seat,"

Momma bargained. "Okay,"

"Yea," London smiled up at her Momma, kissing her on her cheek. "Jayvon hurry up and fall asleep," London laughed.

"Yea right," Jayvon said, rolling his eyes. They all got in the truck and fastened their seatbelts and off they went.

"To infinity and beyond," Asher shouted, sounding like Buzz Lightyear. "We're goin' to start over right Momma?" Jayvon asked. "No," Asher "It's an adventure!" Momma laughed, with tears in her eyes, she refused to let fall.

"You're all right," Momma said, "It's an adventure

filled, new beginning, to infinity and beyond!" They all laughed. AS Momma drove She said, "Jayvon find another radio station, this one's runnin' out." "Okay,"

Jayvon said, searching

for another radio station.

And on every station all

they heard was static. "I

can't find one Momma,"
Jayvon said.

"That's cause we're in the mountains. There should be a country station somewhere on there."

"Momma! You don't listen to country music," he stated.

Momma laughed, "Uh, yea I do. I listen to all kinds of

music. I'm what you call eclectic!" Momma said.

"What's eclectic?" Jayvon asked.

"It just means I'm not forced into one box. I like

a variety. I like a lot of

different things from

different boxes I guess!

You want me to sing a

song?" Momma asked.

"If you want to," Jayvon said, shrugging his shoulders.

"Ooooh I want you to sing Momma," London yelled from the backseat.

Momma glanced back, "I thought yall was sleep! London you wanna sing with me?" Momma asked.

"Oooooh Momma can we sing Pretty Girl Rock?"

"Yea," Momma said. And they sang in unison. "All eyes on me when I walk in, no question that this girl's a 10, don't hate me cause I'm beautiful, don't hate me cause I'm beautiful!" Momma and London sang. "Momma, I already know that song," Jayvon said. "You were supposed to sing an eclectic song." "Okay,"

Momma laughed. "Yall

ready," Momma asked

knowing her voice was

HORRIBLE! "Momma, just

Sing!" Jayvon demanded.

And as their Momma

started to sing they

heard a loud "POP!"

"Momma what was that?"

Jayvon asked. "I don't

know Jayvon," So she kept

driving and all of a sudden the right side of the car was leaning. Momma pulled over and got out to check her tires. "Well," she said, getting back in her truck, "we got a flat tire!" "Oh Noooo!," Asher cried disappointed. "what are we gonna do? We can't just sit here!" Asher said.

"No Asher, I'm gonna call roadside assistance for help," Momma said. Momma grabbed her phone and dialed emergency roadside assistance. "Emergency Roadside Assistance, how can I be of assistance?"

"I'm on 85 North just outside of Charlotte and I caught a flat tire, could you send someone to help me please?" Momma asked. "Sure ma'am," the Operator said. 'Knock, knock,' just then a man was knockin' on Momma's window. Momma rolled her window down and said, "Hi." "Hey Ma'am, I see you got a flat tire, there. You need any help?" the Man asked.   "Yea, actually,

I do." Momma replied. "Well

have you got a spare

tire?" He asked. "I should

have one in the trunk,"

Momma said. "Well pop

your trunk and I'll take a look." the nice man said.

Just then the car raised up, and London jumped! "Momma what was that?" London asked. "He's usin' a jack to lift the car up, so he can take the flat tire off and put on our spare." Momma said. "Oh, COOL!" Asher said. No you're the cool one Momma thought;

always so loving and

kind!

"Momma can I

help?" Jayvon said,

staring out the window

watching the man change the tire. "No Jayvon," She said, "Maybe next time when it's not so dark out."

"All finished," the nice
man said. "Is there
anything else I can do
for you?" "No thank you.
You've saved our lives!"
Momma thanked the nice

man. "Your welcome Ma'am, drive safe. Good night kids." He said. "Good night," Jayvon, London, and Asher yelled in unison. And off he went back to his car. "See it's the small things!" Momma told her kids. "Thank God for men like him," Momma prayed. Momma started the car up and drove up the highway. "Ooohh Momma there's a restaurant! Can we stop, and get something to eat? I'm hungry," London asked. "Yea," Momma said.

"I need a break anyway!

And some hot coffee."

Momma pulled up to the

restaurant and parked.

They ordered blueberry

pancakes, scrambled

eggs with cheese, orange juice, and coffee. Asher made a smiley face on his pancake with whip cream. "Momma look what I made!" Asher said. And they high fived. "Momma lets toast," Jayvon said, raising his cup of orange juice. "To our new life," "That's a great toast Jayvon," Momma said, as they all drank their

orange juice and coffee.

"I've got a good toast

myself," Momma said. "To

the place we are between

our old life and our new

life. The life we can not yet imagine and the life we've already begun to forget!" "I love it!" Asher yelled. After breakfast, the sun was starting to rise, as they got back in their car. "Story time," Momma yelled as they buckled their seat belts and pulled off. "Who has a good story to tell?"

Momma asked. "Momma you go first," Asher demanded. "Okay," Momma said. "I'll tell y'all the story of the Phoenix. Y'all know what a Phoenix is?"

Momma asked. "No," they all said. "A Phoenix is a bird. A huge beautiful bird, with red, orange, yellow, and gold feathers and wings. And Momma

started her story.

"Once upon a time

there was this really

great Mom and her three

really great kids, Jayvon,

London, and Asher. But their Mom was really, really sad, and she wouldn't stop crying. One day Momma walked to get her kids from school.

When they got home, they all stayed outside to play. Then a huge shadow flew over their heads and Momma looked all around to see where the shadow

came from. The kids
didn't even notice the
shadow, so they kept
playing. And the next
thing you know, this huge
bird of beautiful

ravishing red, fiery

orange, and glistening

gold, landed and sat right

next to Momma. And

Momma jumped back

never having seen a

phoenix in real life. The kids didn't know whether to be frightened, or excited. They just stood there, staring with their eyes wide open. But the

Phoenix was crying. And then she spoke, she said, "Excuse me Ma'am I've flown into a tree, and cut my wing. Would you mind helping me sow it back together?" Now Momma

was really frightened,

first a huge Phoenix of

beautiful colors, *AND NOW*

A TALKING PHOENIX, NO A

HUGE TALKING PHOENIX OF

BEAUTIFUL COLORS! Momma just stood there as the Phoenix cried. "Momma!" Jayvon yelled, breaking Momma's trance. "We have to sow her wing, she can't fly without our help." "Just then Momma ran to check the Phoenix's wings. "Jayvon, run in the house and get my needle and thread!"

Momma ordered! And Jayvon ran into their house to get the needle and thread his Momma needed to sow the Phoenix's wing. "Ouch," the Phoenix said, as Momma checked her wing. "This is the first time I cut myself flying. Well, actually, I've never cut myself." The Phoenix remembered. "I'm sorry, I didn't mean to hurt you," Momma said, as she started to sow the Phoenix's wing. When Momma was done, the

Phoenix flew up high towards the sun, then looped around and crash landed. "Ouch," The Phoenix whined. "Maybe that was a little too fast after my first cut. "Are

you ok?" London asked,

the first to run to the

Phoenix's side. "I hope So,"

the Phoenix said. "Well I

will be anyway. I'm always

ok, eventually. And the Phoenix laid her head on the grass and fell fast asleep. "Momma I'm scared," Asher said, "she's crying." And she was. There was one really huge tear running out of the Phoenixs' eye, as she quietly slept. "Don't be scared Asher," Momma kneeled down and gave

Asher a kiss. Then she walked up to the Phoenix to see the tear for herself. Momma reached up and wiped the Phoenixs' tear smoothly

and quietly, as not to
wake her. Then Momma
turned and lift the
Phoenixs' wing to check
her cut. Momma used the
same hand she used to

wipe the Phoenixs' tear,

and the Phoenixs' wing lit

up a glistening gold.

"Wow," Jayvon said.

"Momma what was that?"

He asked.

"I don't know," Momma said. The Phoenix's cut was healed and the thread Momma used to sow the

Phoenix fell to the ground.

"Thank you," the Phoenix said, rising up and checking her wings. "If there is anything I can do for you, please ask."

But Momma couldn't

think of anything. Jayvon,

London, and Asher were

all so excited, they just

wanted to go for a ride;

And Momma just wanted

to go home! But they

were already at home.

But that house wasn't

their home! THEY ALL

HATED IT THERE! So finally

Momma asked the Phoenix. "Will you fly me and my kids to our new home?" "Where's your new home?" The Phoenix asked.

"I don't know," Momma said, ashamed to say. "We'll start at my favorite cousin Deja's house, until we find our own house. She lives in

Syracuse, New York. "Yes,

I'd love to," the Phoenix

said, as they all climbed

on.

"As long as we're

together anywhere is

better than here!" Momma said, not looking back.

And off the Phoenix flew, but before they could get there the Phoenix grew weak and had to land.

Thankfully the Phoenix

landed near a store.

Momma ran to the store

to get the Phoenix Some

water, surely she had to

be dehydrated. When

Momma came back the

Phoenix was nothing but

a huge pile of ashes in

the shape of the

beautiful Phoenix bird

they flew in on.

"Momma," Jayvon said,

"She just went up in

flames! But she was

beautiful the whole time!"

He stated. All three of

them grabbed their

Momma's legs and arms crying for the Phoenix.

"It's okay," Momma said as she turned her kids around to shield them from the ashes. And as they walked toward the store, they heard a small, "chirp!" And they all stopped in their tracks. "Chirp, chirp, chirp." And all three of them turned around at once. "Chirp, chirp," the kids' eyes grew wide at what was before them. "It's a baby," London sang. "Momma look it's a baby Phoenix!

Where did a baby Phoenix come from?" They all wondered. "When it's time for a Phoenix to die they go up in flames." Momma said, "and from their own ashes, they are reborn!"

So Momma picked up the

baby Phoenix, covered

her up, and carried her.

Just as the Phoenix had

carried them! Momma and

her kids all walked to the store for more water and snacks. "Excuse me," Momma said to the cashier. "Is there a hotel near here?" "No! Not for miles, Sorry," the cashier said. Momma paid for their snacks and took her kids outside and they made a picnic. "well," Momma said cradling the sleeping Phoenix, "we can't sit here alday, we have to start walking towards something!" As they started walking the Phoenix became heavy in

Momma's arms. So Momma
decided to take a short
cut through on the trail
beside them. And they
followed the trail
through all of its' twists

and turns and FINALLY

they came upon a cabin!

Momma walked up the

steps and knocked. Then

she waited. And Momma

knocked again, and again

she waited. And Momma

knocked one more time

and the door creaked

open, with a loud and

cranky "CREEEEAAAK!"

"Hello?" Momma yelled

with her head in the
doorway. "Hello? I'm lost.
Is anyone home?" Momma
asked, yelling as she
looked inside. No one was
home, and there was no

furniture, the cabin was completely empty! So they all went in. Momma wanted to start a fire in the fireplace, but she didn't have any matches;

So the baby Phoenix flew

to the fireplace

and breathed her fiery

breath on the fire wood

and "POOF" a fire! After

resting for a while they

were all tired and

hungry. So Momma went

for a walk to think about what she was gonna do, she couldn't walk back to that store, it was *TOO FAR!* Soon she came to a beautiful stream. Momma

turned around and her
kids were right behind
her laughing and running
towards the stream. Then
Momma made a pretend
spear out of twigs and

tried to spear fish, but that didn't work. And they all laughed. So Momma said,

"Jayvon let me borrow your shirt." "Okay,"

Jayvon said, before taking his shirt off, and handing it to Momma. Momma caught a lot of fish with Jayvon's shirt and used her pocket knife to clean them. When they got back to the cabin Momma gave each of her kids a tree branch with a fish on it to roast over the fire. When the fish was done roasting

Jayvon, London, and

Asher ate, then Momma

fed the Phoenix. Then

Momma went back to the

stream to get a fish for

herself. Momma roast, and ate her fish, then they all cuddled under the fire and told stories until they all fell asleep."

"Who wants to guess

what happens next?"

Momma asked, looking at

her kids.

"I know!" Asher yelled,

"And they all lived happily

ever after! The End!"

Asher laughed.

"No," Momma said, "They stayed in the cabin for a few days until the Phoenix grew big enough and strong enough to fly

them home. The End.

Okay, if you gotta use

the bathroom do it now,

cause I'm about to stop

and get some gas," Momma announced. "And you can get one snack a piece." Momma and her kids went in the gas station and paid for their gas and snacks. When they got back in the car Jayvon, London, and Asher all went back to sleep. And Momma found a radio station to keep her company for the rest

of the ride.

THE END

www.ingramcontent.com/pod-product-compliance
Lightning Source LLC
Chambersburg PA
CBHW081943160726
47999CB00008B/2491